THE BOOKS ABOUT ADDY

❋

MEET ADDY · An American Girl

Addy and her mother try to escape from slavery because they hope to be free and to reunite their family.

❋

ADDY LEARNS A LESSON · A School Story

Addy starts her life as a free person in Philadelphia. She learns about reading and writing for the first time—and about the real meaning of freedom.

❋

ADDY'S SURPRISE · A Christmas Story

During the holiday season, Addy and Momma are generous with the little money they've saved—and thrilled by a great surprise.

ADDY
LEARNS
A LESSON
A SCHOOL STORY

By CONNIE PORTER

ILLUSTRATIONS MELODYE ROSALES

VIGNETTES RENÉE GRAEF, JANE S. VARDA

PLEASANT COMPANY

Published by Pleasant Company Publications Incorporated
© Copyright 1993 by Pleasant Company Incorporated
All rights reserved. No part of this book may be used or reproduced in
any manner whatsoever without written permission except in the case of
brief quotations embodied in critical articles and reviews.
For information, address: Book Editor,
Pleasant Company Publications Incorporated,
8400 Fairway Place, P.O. Box 620998,
Middleton, WI 53562.

First Edition.
Printed in the United States of America.
94 95 96 97 98 RND 10 9 8 7 6 5

The American Girls Collection® is a registered trademark of
Pleasant Company Incorporated.

PICTURE CREDITS
The following individuals and organizations have generously given permission to reprint
illustrations contained in "Looking Back": pp. 64-65—The Granger Collection, New York
(segregated school); University of North Carolina—Chapel Hill, Penn School Collection
(woman reading to children); Eleanor S. Brockenbrough Library, The Museum of the
Confederacy, Richmond, VA, Photography by Katherine Wetzel (slave pass for Henry,
assigned by Jefferson Davis, 1808-1889); pp. 66-67—Photographs and Prints Division,
Schomburg Center for Research in Black Culture, The New York Public Library (school
burning); Philadelphia City Archives (school building); pp. 68-69—Oberlin College Archives
(Fanny M. Jackson); Army Military History Institute (school for freedmen); Hargrett Rare Book
and Manuscript Library/University of Georgia Libraries (child teaching woman to read).

Edited by Roberta Johnson
Designed by Myland McRevey and Jane S. Varda
Art Directed by Kathleen A. Brown

Library of Congress Cataloging-in-Publications Data

Porter, Connie Rose, 1959-
Addy learns a lesson : a school story / by Connie Porter ; illustrations by Melodye Rosales ;
vignettes, Renée Graef and Jane S Varda. — 1st ed.
p. cm. — (The American girls collection)
Summary: After escaping from a plantation in North Carolina, Addy and her mother arrive in
Philadelphia, where Addy goes to school and learns a lesson in true friendship.

ISBN 1-56247-078-7 — ISBN 1-56247-077-9 (pbk.)
[1. Fugitive slaves—Fiction. 2. Afro-Americans—Fiction. 3. Friendship—Fiction.
4. United States—History—Civil War, 1861-1865—Fiction.]
I. Graef, Renée. II. Varda, Jane. III. Rosales, Melodye, ill. IV. Title. V. Series.
PZ7.P825Ad 1993 [Fic]—dc20 93-7825 CIP AC

FOR MR. ZIMMERMAN

TABLE OF CONTENTS

ADDY'S FAMILY

POPPA
Addy's father, whose dream gives the family strength.

MOMMA
Addy's mother, whose love helps the family survive.

ADDY
A courageous girl, smart and strong, growing up during the Civil War.

SAM
Addy's fifteen-year-old brother, determined to be free.

ESTHER
Addy's one-year-old sister.

HARRIET DAVIS
*Addy's desk partner,
who has the life Addy
thought freedom
would bring her.*

MISS DUNN
*Addy's kind and
patient teacher, who
doesn't like lines to be
drawn between people.*

SARAH MOORE
*Addy's friend, who
teaches her about
school, the big city, and
true friendship.*

MRS. FORD
*The firm-but-fair
owner of the dress shop
where Momma works.*

MRS. MOORE
*Sarah's mother, who
helps Addy and her
Momma get settled.*

A NEW HOME

Addy Walker and her mother stood
on a busy pier in Philadelphia one hot
afternoon at the end of August.
Addy's boots pinched her toes and trickles of sweat
ran down her back. She took Momma's hand and
looked around nervously. *We finally here,* she
thought. *Momma and me in Philadelphia. We gonna
start our new life here. This where Poppa say freedom is.*

The pier was a noisy place. Huge crates hung
from ropes overhead. They swung by clumsily as
they were unloaded from ships. Addy cringed,
thinking one of the ropes might break and a crate
would come crashing down on her and Momma. A
fishing boat had dumped its catch on the pier. Some

of the fish were still alive. Addy saw their mouths moving as if they were sucking for air. Addy felt the way the fish looked, as though she couldn't breathe in the dirty yellow-gray air that smelled like burning fires.

Addy had never seen so many people in her life. It seemed as if everyone in Philadelphia must be on the pier. Some people bent under the weight of heavy trunks. Others had nothing. Some people stood quietly, looking lost. Others shouted out to people who were meeting them.

"I wish Sam and Poppa was here," Addy said as she saw a small girl being swept up in a man's strong arms.

"Addy, we by ourselves," Momma replied.

"I know, but wouldn't it be something if we was to turn around and they was here, just like magic?" Addy said.

"It would be something," Momma sighed. "I wish I knew where they was."

Addy heard sadness in Momma's voice. Poppa and Addy's brother Sam had been sold off Master Stevens's plantation a few weeks before. Now Poppa and Sam were probably slaves on another plantation—unless they had been able to escape. Momma and Addy had had to leave baby Esther behind when they ran away from Master Stevens's plantation. Esther was too young to make the dangerous escape through the woods with Addy and Momma. Her crying would have given them away. Addy and Momma had spent their days hiding in the woods and traveled only at night when no one would see them. They had finally made it across North Carolina to a hot, crowded boat that took them to Philadelphia.

The boat had just arrived minutes before. Addy felt lost in a sea of strangers. "Momma, you think we should be waiting someplace else?" Addy asked.

"The boat captain said to wait here, Addy," Momma said. "Somebody gonna come for us."

"Maybe we should ask somebody what them signs say," Addy suggested as she looked at signs around the pier.

"We ain't gonna do that," Momma said quickly, with fear in her voice. "We in the big city now, and we can't be trusting strangers."

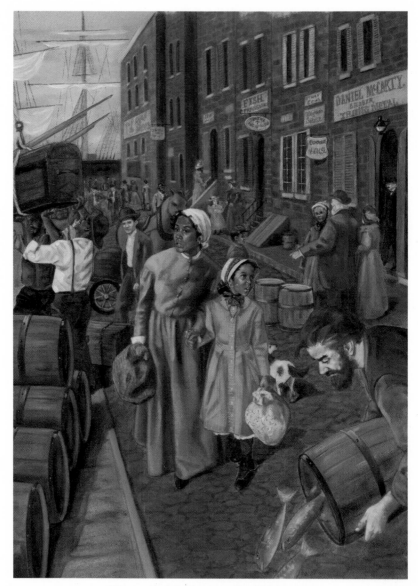

"We in the big city now," said Momma,
"and we can't be trusting strangers."

4

I wish I could read, Addy thought. *Then I could help.* But she did not know one letter. As she shifted back and forth on her aching feet, Addy began to worry.

Maybe no one will come. What if we got to find our way around the city by ourselves? Where we gonna go? Addy's heart started to race, but she tried to keep her face looking calm. She didn't want to worry Momma.

Nearly half an hour passed. The crowd had thinned out when Addy saw a woman and girl coming toward them.

Addy kept her eyes on the girl. She was about Addy's size. She skipped ahead of the woman and waved to Addy as if she were a long-lost friend. As she came closer, Addy saw a sunny smile on her face.

"I'm sorry we late," said the woman, who was tall and heavy-set. She reached out to hug Momma and then Addy. "I was told you was coming on the *Libby,* which is way down on pier thirty-five. Come to find out, you was on the *Liberty* here on pier three. I'm Mabel Moore and this is my girl, Sarah."

Sarah reached out and shook Addy's hand. "It's

good meeting you," she said. Up close, her smile was even brighter.

Mrs. Moore went on, "We from the Freedom Society of Trinity A.M.E. Church, and we gonna take you to the church to see about getting you settled."

"We grateful," Momma said. "I'm Ruth Walker and this is my girl, Addy."

"Well, come on with us," Mrs. Moore said.

As they fell in step behind their mothers, Addy looked shyly at Sarah. Sarah's brown skin was the same color as Addy's. Her hair was as short as a boy's, and her faded dress reminded Addy of the shift she had worn back on the plantation. Sarah's big, dark eyes were so bright, Addy could see herself in them when Sarah turned to her and asked, "Where'd you and your momma come from?"

"North Carolina," Addy answered. "We was slaves on a plantation."

"My family from Virginia. We was slaves, too," Sarah said. "My teacher, Miss Dunn, from North Carolina. Her family was slaves, too."

"They got colored people up here teaching

school?" Addy asked. She could hardly believe it.
Back on the plantation, she didn't know any
colored people who could even read.

"They sure do," Sarah said. "Miss Dunn went
to college and everything. You got to be smart to do
that." Sarah looked at Addy. "You is coming to
school, ain't you?"

"Momma say I can go," Addy answered.

"That's good," said Sarah. "We learn to read
and write. We have spelling matches, learn our
sums, and everything. We even study the war. You
gonna like school. You'll see."

Just then they came to a busy corner. Sarah
took Addy's hand. "I don't want you getting lost
on your first day," she said.

Addy was glad to hold Sarah's hand. She
hardly knew where to look as they walked down
the crowded, narrow streets. She stared at the carts
piled high with fruits and vegetables, heaps of
coal, and bundles of rags. She looked up at the
horse-drawn wagons and carriages that sped past
them. She looked down so that she wouldn't step in
garbage and horse droppings. She stared at all the
people, black and white, old and young. Many of

them wore fine clothes.

Sarah pointed to a street sign. "See that sign there?" she asked Addy. "It tell you where you at. We on Second Street now. When I come up here, I got lost loads of times because I couldn't read."

"Wish I could read," Addy mumbled.

"Not reading is nothing to be 'shamed about," Sarah said, giving Addy's hand a reassuring squeeze. "Miss Dunn will teach you to read. She taught me. And I can help you learn, too."

Addy smiled at Sarah. "I'd like that," she said.

"I'm gonna help you, I promise," Sarah said, smiling her sunny smile.

☀

When they arrived outside the church, Addy was amazed at how big it was. And when they went inside, she could hardly believe her eyes. Addy had never seen such a huge place before. She stood in the middle of the center aisle and slowly turned around.

"That's a pipe organ," Sarah said, pointing to the back of the church. "It make real pretty music. The choir sit up there with it. And look, there in the front of the church. That's the pulpit for the pastor."

"What's that wrote over it?" Addy asked.

"It say, 'Peace be within thy walls,'" Sarah read.

Mrs. Moore led Addy, Momma, and Sarah down to the basement of the church and into a large meeting hall filled with people. The candles in the wall sconces gave the room a warm glow. Long tables were covered with platters of fried chicken, greens, biscuits, pies, and cakes. Addy had seen food like this only once before, a long time ago, when Master Stevens had a grand party. Sarah whispered to Addy that most of the people in the room were church members she knew. But some were slaves who had just arrived from the South. They were new like Addy and Momma. By the time Addy and Momma sat down to eat, it seemed they had been hugged by everyone in the room. Addy felt that they were being welcomed into a big family.

While they were eating, Mrs. Moore asked Momma, "What kind of work can you do?"

"I can sew some," Momma said. "Back on the plantation, I did mostly mending, but sometimes I made shirts and things like that."

Mrs. Moore's face brightened. "I know where you might find some work," she said. "There's a woman over on South Street named Mrs. Ford. She a white woman, and she got a small dress shop. She can be fussy, but she pay good, and I think she got a room you and Addy can stay in."

After the meal, Mrs. Moore left Sarah at the church while she took Addy and Momma to the dress shop just a few blocks away. The tiny shop was crammed with cloth, thread, ribbon, yarn, feathers, and boxes. A woman sat near the back, bent over her sewing. She looked up when they arrived.

"Good day, Mrs. Ford," Mrs. Moore said. The three visitors barely fit inside the shop. Mrs. Moore introduced Addy and Momma and said, "I think Ruth Walker would be a fine seamstress for you."

"I'll be the judge of that," Mrs. Ford snapped, looking over the top of her spectacles. "You know, Mrs. Moore, the last girl you brought here got married and left me soon after she started. I'm an abolitionist and I want to help you colored people. But I have a business to run, and I can't take too many chances."

"Momma a real good sewer," Addy added bravely, "and we ain't gonna take off."

Momma squeezed Addy's arm, and Addy fell silent.

Mrs. Ford's sharp eyes looked at Addy and then at Momma. She said, "I'll hire you, Mrs. Walker—on a trial basis. A dollar a week to start. I run a first-rate shop here. Most of my customers are from Society Hill, and they expect the best. You'll have to do fine work, and I'll expect you to make some deliveries. If you can't do the work, I won't keep you on. This is a business, not a charity ward."

"Yes, ma'am," Momma said. Her voice was soft but steady.

"All right then," said Mrs. Ford. "I'll take you up to the room where you and your daughter can stay."

Addy, Momma, and Mrs. Moore followed Mrs. Ford up three flights of steep, dark stairs. At the top was a garret. Addy's heart sank. The room was dirty, stuffy, and hot. It was smaller than the cabin Addy's family had lived in back on the plantation. A table with two chairs stood in the middle of the room, and a bed had been pushed into one corner. There was a small stove. Then Addy saw something that made her feel better—a window that looked out over the street. Addy's cabin on the plantation had no windows.

"It's not much," Mrs. Ford said. "It's hot in the summer and cold in the winter."

"It'll be fine," Momma said quickly. She put her arm around Addy's shoulders. "We gonna make it a home."

CHAPTER
TWO

FREEDOM?

Addy stood at the window of the
garret, gazing out at the street below.
A week had passed since she and
Momma had arrived in Philadelphia, and nothing
magical had happened at all. Back on the plantation,
Addy had dreamed about being free in the North.
She'd wear fancy dresses, she'd learn to read and
write, she'd spend more time with Momma. She had
imagined that everything would magically be better
when she was free. But so far, freedom wasn't the
way she dreamed it would be.

Momma worked long hours in the shop. She
spent her day making dresses for rich women,
working just as hard as she had on the plantation.

But back there, if Addy didn't have a chore to do, she could find Momma and sit with her while she worked. Not here. Addy had gone down to the shop on Momma's first day. But Mrs. Ford made it clear that Addy was not to be in the shop while Momma was working.

And so Addy spent her days in the hot room in the attic. The window didn't bring Addy much joy. Sometimes a small breeze pushed through it, but the air was foul. Addy could smell soot, rotting garbage from the street, and the fishy scent of the harbor. The window let in all kinds of noises, too. Trains clanked in the distance. Ships in the harbor sounded their deep, lonely horns.

Although Addy didn't like being alone in the room, she was too scared to go out by herself. She didn't know her way around. She couldn't read the street signs, and the crowds of people in the streets frightened her. Sarah had told Addy that she once had seen a boy pushed into the path of a speeding wagon. Both his legs had been crushed.

The only time Addy went downstairs during the day was to go to the
privy. Ten families used the same privy.

privy

14

It sat in the middle of a dark, filthy alley. The privy smelled awful, and the alley did, too. People threw all sorts of things into the alley—dirty water, table scraps. At night, rats prowled through the piles of garbage.

Addy had seen Sarah only once, at church on Sunday. Sarah's mother was a washerwoman and Sarah helped her, so she had little time to play. Addy longed for baby Esther, Sam, and Poppa more than ever, but she didn't tell Momma.

Addy was lost in her thoughts when she heard someone running up the stairs. She opened the door and saw Sarah.

"I'm so glad you here!" Addy exclaimed. "Ain't you got to help your momma today?"

"I do," Sarah said. "She sent me to the store for some bluing and a cake of soap. She said I could stop by here for a minute. And guess what?" Sarah went on. "Your momma said you could come with me."

Addy was so happy, she took Sarah's hand and they ran down the stairs. When they got outside, Sarah said eagerly, "School start next week. I can't wait."

"Me neither," Addy said excitedly.

"You can sit with me," said Sarah. "We got double desks, and you can be my desk partner."

"Good!" agreed Addy, though she couldn't imagine what a double desk looked like.

"My momma is letting me wear my Christmas dress from last year to the first day of school," Sarah went on.

Addy looked down at her dress. It was the same pink one she had worn when Sarah met her at the pier.

"Do the girls dress real fancy at school?" she asked.

"Some do," Sarah answered. "There's this one girl named Harriet. She got lots of pretty dresses."

"It sound like she rich," Addy said.

"Compared to us she is," shrugged Sarah. "Her momma don't work."

They came to a curb and waited for a wagon to go by. It was the biggest one Addy had ever seen. The wagon was drawn by two horses and packed with people, some sitting, some standing.

"What kind of wagon is that?" Addy asked.

"It's a streetcar," Sarah explained. "Streetcars go

all over the city to take
people to different places."

"Let's get on it," Addy said as they crossed the
street. "It look like fun."

"We can't ride it," Sarah said, "even if we had
money for the fare, which we don't."

"You mean children got to ride with their
momma or poppa?" asked Addy.

"No," Sarah said. "I mean they don't let colored
people ride on that streetcar."

Addy looked confused.

"It's true," Sarah said. "There is a few streetcars
for colored people to ride on. But we can only ride
on the outside platform, even if it's raining or
snowing. And they charge us colored folks the same
fare they charge whites."

"That ain't right," Addy said.

"It ain't, but it's the way things is," Sarah said.

☀

When Momma came to bed that night, Addy
told her about the streetcars. "This where freedom
supposed to be at," Addy said. "There ain't
supposed to be things colored folks can't do."

17

"Honey, you right," Momma said, turning over the pillow so the cool side touched Addy's cheek. "But there's more to freedom than riding a streetcar. There ain't nobody here that own us, and beat us, and work us like animals. I got me a paying job. You can go to school and learn to read and write. When you got an education, you got a freedom nobody can take from you. You'll still have it even if you never ride a streetcar."

"I wish you ain't have to work so hard," Addy said. "We got to buy everything now—food, candles, coal, matches. And it all cost so much."

"Freedom got a cost," Momma went on. "Just like Uncle Solomon told us before we left the plantation. It cost money and hard work and heartache." She kissed Addy's forehead. "Be patient, honey. Things gonna get better, I promise. Now, you go on to sleep. I got sewing to do."

☀

The first day of school, Momma and Addy were both up before the sun. Momma had washed, starched, and ironed Addy's pink dress so it looked like new. Now she braided Addy's hair in two braids and tied each with a ribbon that Mrs. Ford had given her from the end of a roll.

When Momma finished, she hugged Addy. "Do good in school now, Addy," she said. "You a smart girl."

"I'm gonna work hard, Momma," Addy replied as she hugged Momma back. Suddenly they heard someone running up the stairs.

Sarah burst into the room without knocking. "You ready, Addy?" she asked. Sarah had on a dark green dress trimmed in white. It was old, but clean and carefully mended.

"You look real nice, Sarah," Momma said. She handed Addy her lunch pail. Momma had tied a scrap of green and white cloth to the pail so Addy could tell hers from other children's. Momma  walked downstairs with the girls. "Y'all be careful now. Watch out for them wagons and streetcars, and don't talk to no strangers. Go straight to school and come right straight back here after."

"Don't worry, Mrs. Walker," Sarah said. She hooked arms with Addy. "I'm gonna look after Addy. I ain't gonna let nothing bad happen to her."

The Sixth Street School was a brick building near Trinity Church. Boys and girls had gathered on the steps out front. All of them were black, and they were all different ages. They were talking and laughing and playing. Addy felt scared, but she tried not to show it. She held tight to Sarah's hand as they walked past the other students and went into the building. Sarah showed Addy the way to their room, which was a classroom for boys and girls in the lower grades.

Addy felt more nervous than ever when she saw the classroom. It was crammed with desks. In one corner was a large black stove. On two walls of the room were huge black squares filled with writing. On another wall there was a large piece of paper filled with colorful shapes. *What's that for?* Addy wondered. A group of children was already in the room, talking happily to one another and looking through books. Addy was worried. She knew those children would soon find out she couldn't read or write. Addy held onto Sarah's hand, but she wanted to break away and run.

Sarah's voice interrupted Addy's thoughts.

"Here come Miss Dunn," Sarah said.

Addy watched as the teacher entered the room. Miss Dunn held her head high and her back straight. Her long skirts swung gracefully as she made her way across the room. She seemed to be gliding on air.

Miss Dunn smiled at Addy and Sarah. "Welcome back, Sarah," she said. "And who is your friend?"

"This here is Addy," Sarah answered. "She from North Carolina just like you, and she ain't never been to school before."

Miss Dunn put her hand on Addy's shoulder. "I'm so pleased you're here, Addy," she said. "You know, I never went to school until my family came north. When I started, some things seemed a little strange. You might feel a bit confused this first week, but you'll soon learn your way. I know Sarah will help you."

Addy smiled as Miss Dunn floated away. The teacher had made her feel much better. Suddenly, a bell rang and more children hurried into the classroom. Addy and Sarah sat down together at a double desk at the back of the room.

*"You might feel a bit confused this first week," said Miss Dunn, "but I
know Sarah will help you."*

When everyone was seated, Miss Dunn said, "Good morning, boys and girls. I am Miss Dunn." She pointed to her name on the blackboard. "I know many of you, but I see some new faces. I want you children who have been here before to help the new students feel a part of our class. If we help each other, I know we will enjoy our year together. Tomorrow I will assign permanent desk partners."

Miss Dunn asked every student to stand up and state his or her name. Then she announced that the class would spend the morning copying from the board. "Sarah," she said, "please help Addy copy the alphabet."

"Yes, ma'am," said Sarah.

Sarah was a patient teacher. She showed Addy how to hold her slate pencil and how to form the letters of the alphabet. Addy tried to hold her pencil the way Sarah did, between her thumb and first two fingers, but it kept slipping. Her letters looked shaky. Addy finally wrapped her entire hand around the pencil. Even then, the letters she slowly formed were squiggly and rough.

Miss Dunn stopped to look at Addy's slate. "You're doing fine," she said. Then she wrote something on one side of the slate. "This is your name," she said. "I want you to practice it."

Addy stared at the letters. It was the first time in her life that she had seen her name written down. Addy tried to copy the letters carefully. But her slate pencil broke because she pressed down so hard. The letters wobbled across her side of the slate in a crooked row. Addy erased them and started again. This time they looked more like Miss Dunn's letters.

Sarah looked at Addy's slate. "That's good, Addy," she said kindly. "I can read that plain as day. A-D-D-Y."

Addy had to smile. It had been a struggle, but she had written her own name, just as she dreamed she would. And she had found something she had not even dreamed of when she worked in the tobacco fields. In Sarah, she had found a friend.

TESTED

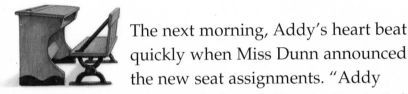

The next morning, Addy's heart beat quickly when Miss Dunn announced the new seat assignments. "Addy Walker, you'll share a desk with Harriet Davis," she said.

Addy and Sarah looked at each other, and then Sarah blurted out, "Miss Dunn, can Addy stay with me? I been helping her."

"No, Sarah, I want Addy to sit near the front of the room. Clara Johnson will be your new desk partner. You can help her," Miss Dunn replied.

Addy rose slowly. She glanced back at Sarah as Clara slid into the seat next to her. Addy went to her new seat. She sat down next to Harriet and smiled shyly. Harriet did not smile back.

Harriet had light brown skin, and she wore her hair loose. She was wearing the most beautiful dress Addy had ever seen. It was light yellow and trimmed with rows of lace. Addy realized that this must be the girl Sarah had told her about.

"Do you know the alphabet?" Harriet asked. She had a thin, high voice.

"I'm just learning it," Addy answered. "Sarah was teaching me."

A quick frown crossed Harriet's face. "Sarah?" she said. "Sarah can hardly read herself! I'll help you. I taught myself to read when I was four. Miss Dunn put you with me because I'm the smartest one in the class."

"Sarah smart, too," Addy responded.

Harriet ignored her comment. "I'm named after Harriet Tubman. She helped run the Underground Railroad. You probably didn't know that. I know plenty of things like that. Now that Miss Dunn put you with me, I can teach you some things."

At lunch Sarah asked, "How you like sitting with Harriet?"

"She real smart and she got fine clothes just like

"Miss Dunn put you with me because I'm the smartest one in the class," said Harriet.

you said. I wish I had a dress as pretty as the one she has on," Addy said.

"You know how much one of them fancy dresses cost?" Sarah asked.

"How much?" Addy asked.

"More than my momma and poppa make in a whole month," Sarah answered. "Your momma can't afford to make you a dress like that, Addy."

Addy's eyes opened wide. She had no idea one dress could cost so much. "Maybe my momma can find a way," she said. "Harriet's momma could afford it."

"I'm sick of talking about Harriet," Sarah snapped.

Addy was surprised by Sarah's reaction. "What's the matter?" she asked. "Don't you like her?"

"That ain't it," Sarah said, letting out a sigh. "Addy, Harriet don't like me. She all stuck-up. She think she better than other people. If your family ain't got no money, she don't like you. And you know my family poor."

"But Harriet was nice to me," Addy protested, "and she know my family is poor."

"Listen, Addy. She was only nice 'cause

Miss Dunn told her to be," Sarah said firmly.
"Harriet don't have no poor girls like us for her
friends. She gonna try to make you her slave. She
tried it with me when I came to school last year, but
I wouldn't let her. That's why she don't like me. She
gonna hurt you just like she hurt me last year."

"Well, maybe Harriet changed from when you
first come up here," Addy said. "Harriet ain't gonna
hurt me. She say she got plenty to teach me, and I
got plenty to learn."

As the weeks passed, Addy's fascination with
Harriet grew. Every day Harriet wore a beautiful
dress. Each one seemed brand new. And schoolwork
came so easily to Harriet! She was always the first
one in the class to finish her lesson, so she had time
to look at Addy's slate and point out Addy's
mistakes. Sometimes Addy didn't understand the
corrections Harriet made. But questions seemed to
annoy Harriet, so Addy saved her questions to ask
Sarah at lunchtime or when they walked home
together after school.

Addy worked very hard, and so she was
discouraged after her first spelling test. Out of the
twenty words on the test, Addy spelled twelve

wrong. When Miss Dunn handed back
Addy's test at the end of the day, she was
encouraging. "Look how many words you got right,
Addy. If you keep learning this fast, you'll be one of
the best spellers in the class. Maybe your mother
could help you with the words you missed."

"Yes, ma'am," Addy said softly. She didn't want
to tell Miss Dunn that Momma couldn't read or
write. And she didn't want Harriet to overhear her
say it.

When Addy and Sarah were walking home after
school, Addy said, "I ain't never gonna catch up.
Younger girls can read and spell better than me.
Maybe it's too late for me to learn."

"It ain't never too late," said Sarah. "You can't
learn everything at once. Learning go slow. I didn't
do so good on the test, neither. I should've studied
harder."

"I studied hard and I still didn't do good,"
Addy said. "How many did you get right?"

"How many did you get right?" Sarah asked.

"I asked first," Addy said.

Sarah said, "Well, I got 'em all wrong 'cause I
didn't study at all. My poppa can't hardly find

work, so my momma and me been taking in extra washing. Sometimes I ain't got time to do my lessons."

"Maybe we can do our lessons together sometime," Addy said.

"I'd like that," Sarah said, sounding more cheerful.

Sarah left Addy at the door of Mrs. Ford's shop, and Addy stepped inside. As she headed toward the stairs, she saw Momma sitting in the back of the shop. She was crying. "Momma, what's the matter?" Addy asked.

Momma dried her eyes on the sleeve of her dress. "You can come in, Addy," she said. "Mrs. Ford ain't here. She went out and left these packages for me to deliver. She wrote down the addresses on this here paper. I ain't dare tell her I can't read. She gonna be coming back soon expecting to see these packages gone, but I don't know where to take them."

"I can take them," Addy said. She  looked at the addresses, but her heart sank when she realized she could read only one of them. Then an idea came to her.

"Momma, Sarah can help. She can read way better than me, and she know her way around Philadelphia."

Momma looked doubtful.

"Momma, let me go catch up with Sarah. It's the only way," Addy begged.

"All right," Momma said after a moment. "But y'all be extra careful."

Addy grabbed the packages and paper and started running. She caught up with Sarah a few blocks away and explained the problem. Sarah studied the paper for a moment. Then she said, "I know where these streets is. Let's go."

Sarah hurried through the busy streets with Addy rushing along beside her. Sarah pointed to the street signs and read the names aloud for Addy. She showed her how the numbers on the houses went in order. After they had delivered the last package, the girls walked back to the shop.

As they walked in the door, Momma threw her arms around them. "Sarah, you been a big help. I don't know what we'd do without you," she said.

Just then Mrs. Ford returned. When she saw
Addy and Sarah, she said, "What's going on here,
Mrs. Walker? This is a place of business, you know."

"Yes, ma'am. The girls were just leaving,"
Momma said quickly. She squeezed Sarah's hand to
thank her again. Sarah headed for home, and Addy
hurried up the stairs to the garret.

That evening, as Momma was cooking supper,
she sounded worried. "I ain't got a right to this job
because I ain't been honest with Mrs. Ford. I gotta
learn to read or find something else to do."

"Momma, I can teach you how to read!" Addy
exclaimed.

Momma shook her head. "I think it's too late for
me," she said.

"Sarah say it ain't never too late," said Addy.
She took her spelling paper out of her satchel. "I got
most of them wrong," she said, showing the paper
to Momma. "But Miss Dunn say if you help me, I
could be one of the best spellers at school."

"But I don't know how to help you, Addy,"
Momma replied. "I don't know the letters."

"I can teach them to you," Addy answered,
"and I'll get practice from helping you."

Momma's eyes looked for a moment at the cowrie shell hanging around Addy's neck. Momma had given Addy the shell when they were escaping the plantation. It came from Addy's great-grandmother, who had been captured in Africa and brought to America as a slave. "All right, Addy. I'll try," Momma said. "Our family done faced tougher things than this. Ain't no change coming overnight, but by and by maybe we'll both learn."

Addy smiled at Momma. "Let's have our first lesson tonight."

☀

As the weeks passed and it started to get cool, Momma kept a small fire in the stove in the evenings. Sometimes when they made bread or meat pies for supper, Addy showed Momma how to spell words by forming letters with scraps of leftover dough. Momma loved to write *Sam*, *Poppa*, and *Esther*. "Seeing their names make me feel closer to them," she said. After they ate, they went over Addy's lessons. Addy taught Momma how to count, showing Momma what she had learned on the abacus at school by using beans on the table.

abacus

Every day Addy and Sarah went back and forth
to school together, sometimes stopping to pick up
colorful leaves or smooth chestnuts that fell from the
trees. Sarah taught Addy how to read the names on
street signs and shops as they walked along. One
brisk morning as they passed by a grocery store,
Addy stopped to read the sign. "Wil-son Bro-thers
Gro-cer-y. Eggs forty-eight cents a dozen."

"That's right," Sarah said. "You getting real
smart."

"You been a good teacher," Addy said, smiling
at her friend. "But you and me not as smart as

Harriet. You should see her papers. All 100s. She already doing multiplication."

Sarah didn't say anything. She turned her head to look at a shop window.

"Did you see that blue dress Harriet had on yesterday?" Addy sighed. "It was *so* pretty. I never even seen her in it before. She must have ten or fifteen dresses."

"Let's talk about something else," Sarah cut in. "I don't like talking about her, or even thinking about her."

But Addy liked thinking about Harriet. Harriet had everything that Addy had dreamed freedom would bring *her*. Harriet had fancy dresses. Harriet was smart. Harriet was sure of herself. When they were at their desk together, Harriet helped Addy with her schoolwork. But Harriet never invited Addy to be part of her group. Harriet had many friends. Her friends wore fancy dresses and matching hair ribbons. They buzzed around Harriet as if she were a queen bee. They ate lunch together and played at recess. Addy and Sarah walked home the same way Harriet and her friends did, but Addy and Sarah were never asked to join them.

One day at the end of October, Harriet and her friends were walking home just ahead of Addy and Sarah. Addy started walking faster.

"What you hurrying up for?" Sarah asked sharply.

Addy whispered back, "Let's catch up with them."

"You can if you want," Sarah answered, "but I ain't walking with them."

"Aw, come on. We all going the same way," Addy said softly, catching hold of Sarah's arm.

"I said I ain't walking with them," Sarah repeated loudly.

Harriet stopped and turned around. "I heard you, Sarah," she snapped. "Nobody *asked* you to walk with us." Harriet smiled a cool smile at Addy. "But *you* can come with us if you want, Addy."

Addy got a warm, excited feeling. She turned to look at Sarah, but Sarah wouldn't look at her. Sarah looked down at her scuffed boots. Addy didn't know what to do. She knew she would hurt Sarah if she went with Harriet.

"Sarah isn't the boss of you," Harriet said in a loud voice as Addy hesitated. "You can walk with us whenever you want, Addy. It's your decision." Harriet gave Sarah a nasty look, and then she and her friends disappeared around the corner.

THE LINES ARE DRAWN

That evening, Addy was studying her spelling words as Momma made supper. Momma sprinkled flour on the table and began rolling out a piece of dough. She was making biscuits to go with their supper of black-eyed peas. Addy gathered scraps of dough as Momma began cutting the biscuits.

"One word I been wanting to learn to spell is *family*," Momma said to Addy. "You know how to spell that word yet?"

"I do," Addy answered. She started working the scraps of dough into thin strips and made an *F* and then an *A*. "Momma, what do you think Esther doing right now?" Addy asked as she continued making the letters.

"I suspect she getting ready to eat her supper, too," Momma said.

"I miss her," Addy said, "and Poppa and Sam." She sighed deeply. "Momma, when we gonna live together again like a real family?"

Momma sighed, too. "I can't say when we'll be together again, Addy," she said. "But I don't want you thinking that we ain't a family 'cause we ain't all in one place. We just as much a family as we was back in North Carolina."

Addy finished spelling *family* with the dough pieces.

"F-A-M-I-L-Y," Momma read. "Family, that's us."

"That's us," Addy smiled softly.

☀

The next day in school, Miss Dunn talked about the war and about the progress the soldiers from the North were making. "It appears that our Union troops are winning the war," she said proudly.

The class cheered.

Miss Dunn went on. "Now, it's important for

the Union soldiers to know we support them."

Harriet interrupted. "My mother does volunteer nursing to help wounded colored soldiers," she said importantly. "She says many of the soldiers she sees are missing an arm or a leg."

Some of the children groaned. "I'm sure that's true," Miss Dunn said. "This has been a very bloody war. The soldiers who make it back alive are lucky, even those who are missing limbs. Many soldiers are dying in battle. All of the men who go off to fight for the North are our heroes. They need to know we care about them. That's why the whole school is going to the Baltimore Depot today to help send off a troop of colored soldiers."

An excited buzz went through the room.

"I wish I was old enough to fight," Billy Maples blurted out. "Even if I lost a leg, I'd still be a hero."

Sarah raised her hand. "Miss Dunn, why there got to be a war at all?" she asked.

Miss Dunn paused for a moment. "Sometimes people fight even when they don't want to. They fight for what they believe is right," she said.

"I still wish there wasn't no war," Sarah said.

Before Miss Dunn could respond to her, Harriet

turned around in her seat and said to Sarah, "You
know the war is going to free the slaves. You should
be glad for the war. *You* were a slave yourself."

"Harriet, that will be enough," Miss Dunn said.
"Almost all of us colored people used to be slaves."

"Not me. My family has always been free,"
Harriet said proudly.

Addy could see a tense look come over Miss
Dunn's face.

"Girls and boys, almost all colored people came
to America as slaves," she said. "If you weren't a
slave, someone in your family probably was. One of
the reasons there is a war now is because a line
exists between colored and white people. That line
is slavery." Miss Dunn turned and faced Harriet.
"We don't need to do or say anything that draws
more lines between people. The entire country has
been divided in two. Let's not make differences
based on who was a slave or wasn't, or *anything*
else. Is that clear, class?"

"Yes, Miss Dunn," came the answer from all the
students together.

"Harriet," Miss Dunn said sharply, "do I make
myself clear?"

"Yes, ma'am," Harriet mumbled, embarrassed.

"Good," said Miss Dunn. "When we go to the depot, I want you all to be on your best behavior. Now line up with your desk partners."

As the class left the building, Harriet put her arm around Addy's shoulders. "So what did you decide?" Harriet asked. "Are you walking home with me and my friends today after school, or do you have to ask Sarah's permission?"

"I don't have to ask her permission," Addy said quickly. "I'm gonna walk with you."

"Good," Harriet said. She sounded satisfied.

By the time the students arrived at the railroad station, a crowd had gathered. The students lined up along the street with the other people to watch the soldiers march by straight and tall in their blue uniforms trimmed with brass buttons. Addy and her class cheered and applauded, but as Addy looked around, she saw that not everyone was cheering. Some women and children were crying as they watched the soldiers march off to war. Then Addy saw one soldier who looked like her brother Sam. Suddenly she felt like crying herself. Addy turned to Harriet and said, "My brother

The students watched the soldiers march by straight and tall.

wanted to fight in the war."

"Really?" replied Harriet. She didn't sound interested. "My uncle is serving with the 3rd Infantry. That was the first colored regiment organized in the state."

"Oh," said Addy. She wished she knew as much about where Sam was as Harriet knew about her uncle.

On the way back to school, the boys marched straight and tall just as the soldiers had, and the class sang "Rally 'Round the Flag."

When school ended that day, Addy gathered her lunch pail and books and went to Sarah's desk. "I'm gonna walk with Harriet and her friends today," Addy said firmly. "She asked me. You can come too if you want."

"No, I can't," Sarah said, her voice shaking.

Addy could see that Sarah was hurt. She was starting to say something to Sarah when she heard Harriet call, "Come on, Addy." Addy turned to see Harriet surrounded by her friends. She gestured for Addy to come.

"Go on," Sarah said bitterly. "You know you want to."

Without looking at Sarah, Addy ran to join Harriet. Once she caught up with Harriet and her friends, she glanced back at Sarah, who was alone. Addy felt torn, but Harriet distracted her.

"How do you think you'll do in the spelling match on Friday?" Harriet asked Addy.

"I hope I'm gonna do all right," Addy replied. "I been studying real hard."

"Can you believe Miss Dunn gave us 75 words to learn?" asked Mavis, one of Harriet's friends. She was a tall girl with sandy brown hair.

"Harriet is going to win," another girl said. "She doesn't even have to study."

Addy looked back over her shoulder again for Sarah. But Sarah had disappeared.

"We've been going to my house after school to study for the spelling match," Harriet said. "Maybe you can come with us sometime, Addy. Here." Harriet handed Addy her books. One by one, the other girls piled their books on top.

"These are kinda heavy," Addy said. "Why I got to carry them all?"

"Well, if you want to be with us, you have to be our flunky," Harriet said.

"What's that?" Addy asked, struggling with the books.

Harriet and her friends giggled.

"Oh, Addy, I can tell that you just got off the plantation," said Harriet.

She cast a sly look at Mavis and then said to Addy, "You have to be a flunky because you are the new girl. It's sort of like you have to pass a test to be friends with us."

"What kinda test?" Addy asked.

"Oh, I can't tell you too much. That would be cheating," Harriet said.

The girls all laughed again, and Addy felt too embarrassed to ask more. She felt that the girls all had a secret that they weren't sharing with her.

When the group reached Mrs. Ford's shop, the girls quickly took their books off Addy's pile.

"I'll see y'all tomorrow," Addy called as they walked away.

"Bye," Harriet called, not bothering to look back at Addy.

Inside the shop, Momma and Mrs. Ford were busily working.

"Good afternoon, Mrs. Ford," Addy said. "I know this is a place of business, but can I talk to Momma for a minute?"

"Make it quick," Mrs. Ford said, never looking up from her work.

"Momma, can I go to Harriet's house to study for the spelling match?" Addy asked. "I told you about her before. She my desk partner, and she invited me."

"I suppose it'd be fine," Momma answered, "but only if Sarah go with you."

Addy suddenly felt sick to her stomach. Harriet would never include her if Sarah had to come along.

"Where *is* your friend?" Mrs. Ford asked.

Addy looked away. "She ain't want to walk with me today," she said.

"That don't sound like Sarah," Momma said, surprised.

"It's true, Momma," Addy said quickly. "Anyhow, I know my way around now."

As Addy slowly climbed the long stairs to the garret, she tried to convince herself that what she had just told Momma *was* true. Sarah had *not* wanted to walk with her today. She also tried to figure out a way she could go to Harriet's without Sarah. Addy knew a line had been drawn between Sarah and Harriet and neither one would cross it.

CHAPTER
FIVE
—

THE SPELLING
MATCH

The next morning, Addy and Sarah walked most of the way to school in silence. Finally Addy asked, "You angry with me?"

"I ain't angry," Sarah said.

They walked the rest of the way to school without talking. As soon as they arrived, Addy hurried to her desk. Harriet was already sitting there.

"My momma say I could come to your house to study," Addy said happily.

"Really," Harriet said. She sounded cool. "I'm sure you have lots of studying left to do, but I don't really need to study anymore."

"I been studying real hard," Addy said. "We could help each other."

"Well, maybe," Harriet said.

All day Addy felt jumpy with excitement. She couldn't keep her mind on her work. She kept thinking about the fine house Harriet must have, filled with dolls and other toys. Maybe Harriet would let her play with them this afternoon.

When the day was finally over, Sarah came up to Addy. "You ready to walk home?" she asked.

"Well . . . I'm walking with Harriet," Addy said. "I'm going to her house."

"Fine," Sarah said flatly. "Go with her. I don't care." Her voice did not waver this time. She turned away from Addy.

"Sarah," Addy began. But Harriet's friends surrounded her. The girls dumped their books in Addy's arms again. They were every bit as heavy as the water bucket she used to carry back on the plantation. But Addy didn't complain. At last, she was going to Harriet's house.

"Did you see Sarah today?" Harriet said in a mean voice. "Her dress was so wrinkled, it looked like she slept in it."

Mavis added, "And she had a big brown stain on the front of it."

"Her mother is a washerwoman, and she can't even keep Sarah's clothes clean," said Harriet.

All the girls laughed, except Addy. "That's not funny," she said. "Her momma work hard."

"She must not be working hard enough, because Sarah is a mess," Harriet said.

"That don't matter," Addy said softly.

Harriet said, "Of course it matters. Anyway, what do you care about Sarah, Addy? You're on our side now. At least your mother keeps you looking presentable, even if you do wear that same old dress every day. Don't you have any others?"

"No," Addy said, swallowing hard.

"Addy looks good enough to be our flunky, though," Mavis said.

The girls all giggled. "That's true," Harriet said lightly. "Sarah didn't. But you, Addy, are a perfect flunky."

Addy smiled weakly, but she had a sick feeling in her stomach.

When the girls reached Mrs. Ford's shop, Harriet suddenly took her books from the pile Addy was carrying. Addy was confused. "Hey, I can go with y'all today," she said. "I can study at your house, Harriet."

"I don't think so. Not today," Harriet said.

"But the spelling match is tomorrow," Addy protested.

Harriet shrugged, "Well, maybe you can come someday, but not today," she repeated. "Come on," she said to the other girls. They grabbed their books and hurried away, leaving Addy alone at the shop door.

Addy stood there, unable to move. Finally, she

ran up to the garret and threw herself on the bed.
Her face burned as if she had been stung by a
swarm of bees. Sarah had been right. Harriet did
not want Addy to be her friend. She just wanted
Addy to be her slave. And even worse, Addy had
chosen to be her slave. Addy reached for the cowrie
shell Momma had given her and cried with shame.

The next day was the day of the spelling match.
When Addy woke up, Momma was already at the
stove stirring a pot of grits. Addy got up and
washed in a small basin beside the bed. She looked
for the pink dress that Momma always
laid out over the back of her chair, but her
dress wasn't there. In its place was a blue
skirt and jacket trimmed in black braid
and a crisp white shirt. Addy stood
staring at them.

"I made them out of some leftover
cloth from the shop. I want you to look your best
for that spelling match," Momma said, smiling.
"You surprised?"

"Oh, Momma, thank you," Addy said, throwing

her arms around Momma. "They nicer than anything I ever dreamed about."

Momma took the clothes off the chair and helped Addy dress. "I been staying up late for weeks now working on them, hoping I could surprise you," said Momma, fastening the skirt. When Momma stood back to admire Addy in her new clothes, her dark eyes sparkled with pride. "Look at you! You look like a fancy city girl," Momma said. "No matter how you do in the spelling match, I'm gonna be proud of you. You done worked real hard."

But as Addy walked to school that morning in her new outfit, she didn't feel she deserved the new clothes. Once she got to school, the hours dragged by slowly. Addy became more and more nervous during the morning lessons. When the spelling match finally started, her stomach felt queasy.

Harriet was given the first word to spell— *carriage.* She rattled off the letters quickly, "C-A-R-R-I-A-G-E."

"Correct," Miss Dunn said. "Sarah, you have the next word. Spell *button.*"

"B-U-T-T-O-N," Sarah spelled in a soft voice.

"Correct," said Miss Dunn. "Addy, it's your turn. Spell *tomorrow.*"

Addy started to spell quickly, just as Harriet had. "T-O-M-O-R-O-," but then she stopped. This was one of the words she had trouble spelling. She stopped and thought. She knew she could spell this word. She started again, this time more slowly, "T-O-M-O-R-R-O-W."

"Correct," Miss Dunn said.

Addy breathed a sigh of relief. At least she wouldn't make a mistake in the first round of the spelling match.

Harriet leaned over and whispered, "I'm going to win, and my mother said I can have friends over after school for ice cream to celebrate. She said I could bring five girls. I might ask you."

Addy said nothing. Her stomach felt worse.

After two rounds, half the class had missed a spelling word and had to sit down. Addy was glad that Sarah was still in the contest.

Sarah's next word was *account.*

Sarah began, "A-C-C-," and then she paused.

Addy closed her eyes. *O-U-N-T,* she thought. *Come on, Sarah, you can spell it. A-C-C-O-U-N-T.*

Sarah began again, "A-C-C-O-N-T," she said.

"I'm sorry," Miss Dunn said. "That's not correct."

Addy's turn was next. She took a deep breath. She knew how to spell the word, but she didn't want to hurt Sarah anymore. She decided she would spell it wrong on purpose to apologize to Sarah.

But before Miss Dunn called on Addy, Harriet whispered to her again. "I can't believe Sarah missed such an easy one," she said. "She is so dumb."

Addy felt a flash of anger. *I'll show her*, Addy thought. When Miss Dunn called on her, Addy spelled the word correctly.

The spelling match went into the third round. Addy spelled *bridge* correctly. In the fourth round, she got *scissors* right. When the fifth round came, there were two spellers left, Harriet and Addy.

Harriet had the first word. "*Principle*," Miss Dunn said. "We all live our lives by principles. *Principle*."

"P-R-I-N-S-I-P-L-E," Harriet said quickly.

"I'm sorry," Miss Dunn said. "That is not correct."

The students started talking among themselves.

"Quiet," Miss Dunn demanded. "Give Addy a chance to think in peace. Addy, you must spell the word correctly to win. *Principle.*"

Slowly and deliberately, Addy spelled out the letters, "P-R-I-N-C-I-P-L-E."

"Correct!" Miss Dunn exclaimed. She beamed with delight as she said, "Addy Walker, you have truly earned this prize."

 Miss Dunn came over to Addy and pinned a medal on her jacket. "Your hard work has paid off," she said. "Class, please clap for Addy." The boys and girls clapped and cheered.

It was time for lunch by then, and Miss Dunn announced that the class could eat outside because it was a warm day. Several girls rushed up to Addy to congratulate her before they left the classroom.

Harriet stood at the edge of the group. "Well," she said briskly. "If I had studied at all, I would have beaten you. Anyway, Miss Dunn gave you easier words."

"You're just jealous, Harriet," Mavis said. "Addy spelled the word *you* missed."

Slowly and deliberately, Addy spelled out the letters,
"P-R-I-N-C-I-P-L-E."

"I'm not jealous of her," Harriet shrugged.

But Mavis was saying to Addy, "You have on such a pretty new outfit. Where did your mother buy it?"

"She ain't buy it, she made it," Addy answered.

"It's so nice," Mavis said, touching the braid on the jacket. "I wish my mother could sew like this."

Harriet cut into the conversation, "We're eating out on the front steps if you want to join us," she said to Addy. "Come on, girls."

Addy watched as Harriet and her friends went outside. Then she sat down at her desk, pretending she was looking for something inside it. She felt a hand on her shoulder. It was Miss Dunn.

"This is a very special day for you, Addy. Why are you in here all by yourself?" the teacher asked.

Addy kept rooting through her desk.

"I don't think you'll find what you're looking for inside that desk, Addy," Miss Dunn said.

Addy still did not look up.

Miss Dunn reached for Addy's hand. "Addy, look at me," she said gently. Addy slowly looked up. "I suspect you're feeling bad because lines have been drawn between some girls in this class."

"Miss Dunn," Addy said, "I don't know how to get rid of the lines. I done hurt Sarah, and I wouldn't blame her if she never spoke to me again."

"We all make mistakes," Miss Dunn said. "I suspect you've learned a lesson about friendship. But you can't make things better by hiding in here. You need to think about what you stand for and *act* on it." Miss Dunn smiled at Addy and then left her alone.

Addy took her lunch pail from the floor, opened the lid, and looked to see what Momma had packed. When she saw what was on top, she closed the lid and hurried out of the classroom. Addy went around to the side of the building. She stopped when she saw Sarah sitting alone under a small tree. Addy took a deep breath. Then she walked up to Sarah and knelt beside her.

"I'm so sorry, Sarah," Addy said. "Please forgive me. I wanted to be friends with Harriet because she was popular and smart and rich. But she ain't a real friend. I know you is. I never meant to hurt you. I want you to still be my friend."

"I still want to be your friend," Sarah said,

smiling that sunny smile Addy had seen the first day she and Momma had arrived at the pier. Then Sarah reached out and touched Addy's medal.

"I wanted you to win so bad," Sarah said.

"I wanted you to win, too. I was sad when you missed your word," Addy said. "Maybe we can study spelling together right now." She reached into her lunch pail. There on top were four cookies Momma had made, each in the shape of a letter. L-O-V-E.

"Here," Addy said, holding the cookies on her outstretched hand. "This is our first word."

**LOOKING
BACK
1864**

A Peek Into
the Past

A school for newly freed people.

From America's earliest days to the time when Addy was growing up, it was very difficult for African Americans—especially enslaved African Americans—to get an education. Black children were not allowed to attend the earliest American schools at all, although some still learned to read and write. Sometimes they learned from whites who wanted them to read the Bible or do work that required reading and writing. Blacks who did learn how to read and write often taught others. By the mid-1700s, a few churches and some individuals also opened schools for black children.

A white teacher turning black children away from school.

Some owners read the Bible to their slaves.

By the 1830s, it was against the law in most southern states to teach African Americans to read and write. Many whites didn't want blacks to be able to read about freedom in the North because they were afraid their slaves would run away. They didn't want them to write either because then they would be able to write notes called *passes* that said they were free to leave the plantations. People who were caught teaching African Americans to read could be put in prison or forced to pay large fines. Black people who were caught learning to read and write might be whipped or punished in some other way.

Even though it was dangerous, many black children in the South secretly learned to read and write. Some

A pass like this one allowed slaves to leave the plantations where they lived.

children had their lessons at night after working hard all day. Others traded something for lessons. For example, one enslaved boy who was a good marble player helped a white boy learn to play marbles. The white boy then taught him about the alphabet. Slave children might hide under an open window outside a school to listen and learn whatever they could. Some slave owners ignored the laws and taught their slaves to read and write anyway. Sometimes a slave owner's wife or children taught slaves, without the owner knowing about it.

Even in the North where there was no slavery, schooling for black children was poor. Some cities began to have public schools for all children, but usually black students were taught in separate schools from white students, just as Addy was. This separation is called *segregation*. Schools for black children had few supplies and poor buildings compared with those for white children.

Some African-American parents paid tutors to teach their children rather than send them to the crowded public schools for blacks. In Philadelphia and many

Some schools for blacks, even in northern free states, were attacked by angry whites who did not want blacks to get an education.

One of Philadelphia's separate public schools for blacks in the 1800s.

other northern cities, some African Americans had their own small schools in homes or churches that were often better than the segregated public schools.

During Addy's time, the school year in Philadelphia began in the fall and ended in May or June. Schools taught reading, writing, spelling, grammar, geography, arithmetic, and sometimes American history. Students sometimes used an abacus to learn arithmetic. Some schools also taught music and drawing, as well as sewing and knitting for girls. Many schools began to place students in different grades, too.

In all schools of the time, teachers emphasized patriotism, duty to God and parents, thrift, order, cleanliness, and obedience. During the war years, northern schools often started or ended the day with a patriotic song. "America" and "Rally 'Round the Flag" were very popular.

Black parents in the North wanted black teachers to teach in their public schools, but there were few African-American teachers

A page from an 1862 school reader.

162   SANDERS' UNION READER.

LESSON XLIII.

Frown, express displeasure.	Pos sess', have; own.
Ex press', utter; declare.	For sake', abandon.
Wrong'ed, injured.	Deem, think; judge. [dates.
Scorn'ed, despised.	Pre' cepts, commands; man-
Cus' tom, usage.	Con' science, sense of right and
Price' less, invaluable.	wrong.

DARE AND DO.

1. Dare to think, though others frown;
    Dare in words your thoughts express;
    Dare to rise, though oft cast down;
    Dare the wronged and scorned to bless.

2. Dare from custom to depart;
    Dare the priceless pearl possess;
    Dare to wear it next your heart;
    Dare, when others curse, to bless.

3. Dare forsake what you deem wrong;
    Dare to walk in wisdom's way;
    Dare to give where gifts belong;
    Dare God's precepts to obey.

4. Do what conscience says is right;
    Do what reason says is best;
    Do with all your mind and might;
    Do your duty, and be blest.

Questions.—What should we *dare?* What ought we to *do?*

until after the Civil War. Philadelphia's Institute for Colored Youth was the country's first high school for African Americans. People like Miss Dunn were educated there.

During the Civil War, many slaves ran away to freedom or were set free by Union troops. These newly freed slaves were called *freedmen*. Churches and other groups in the North began to send teachers, both black and white, to teach the freedmen. Schools were set up wherever space could be found—in houses, sheds, or stables—until regular schools could be built. At first there were not enough supplies or desks.

Fanny M. Jackson taught at the Institute for Colored Youth from 1865 to 1902.

A school for freedmen. Former slaves of all ages wanted to learn to read and write.

Some children studied together outdoors if there was no school for them to attend.

African-American adults and children flocked to these schools in the South, though they often faced anger and even threats to their lives from whites who wanted blacks to stay uneducated and enslaved. The schools were successful mostly because of the efforts of African Americans themselves. They took risks, made sacrifices, and gave the schools whatever money or goods they could so they could get an education.

By the time Addy was in school, thousands of blacks had learned to read and write. They knew that education meant true freedom—that education opened the door to better jobs and better lives.

Some children taught their parents, who as slaves were not allowed to get an education.

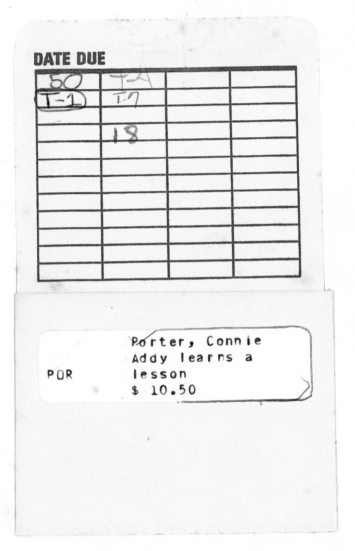

DATE DUE

50			
T-1	T-7		
	18		